Freddy the

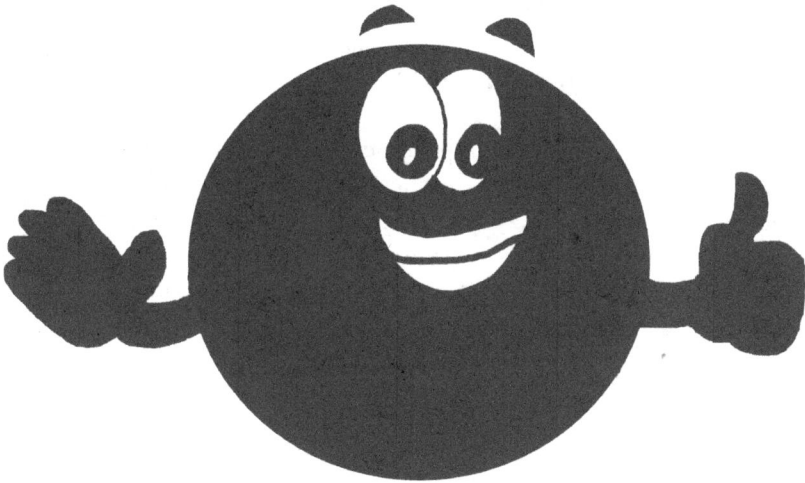

Written by Gabrielle Begun

Illustrated by Novella Genelza

Text Copyright © 2014 Gabrielle Begun
Illustrations Copyright © 2014 Novella Genelza
Cover Design, Interior Design, and Logo by Novella Genelza
Editor-in-Chief: Novella Genelza
Editors: Carter Jung, Jyoti Yelagalawadi, and Keith White
Typeset in Times New Roman and KG No Regrets

ISBN: 978-1-937675-11-0

Published in the United States by:
Lekha Publishers LLC.
4204 Latimer Avenue, San Jose, CA 95130
www.LekhaInk.com

Table of Contents

Chapter 1: Freddy.. 6

Chapter 2: The Fountain... 11

Chapter 3: A Leap of Faith.. 19

Chapter 4: Flying... 23

Chapter 5: The State Capitol.. 27

Chapter 6: Washington, D.C... 32

Chapter 7: The Leader of the Golden Coins................. 36

Chapter 8: Family.. 40

Prologue

Most people think that pennies are not very valuable or interesting coins, but they are wrong. Here is a story about a penny that just might change the way you look at those little copper coins forever...

Chapter 1: Freddy

One day, a shining copper penny jumped out of a coin factory. "Look out, world! Here I come!" Freddy exclaimed with excitement as he rolled off of the assembly line and onto the ground. A man began to walk towards him and stooped down to scoop Freddy up. "I'm hitching my first ride! Oh, I can't wait!" Freddy cried as he fell into the man's pocket. It was very dark inside the sewn fabric. Freddy squinted, and whispered to himself, "Where am I?"

"I hear another voice," replied another penny. She rolled out of the shadows.

"Who are you?" Freddy quickly replied, adding, "You are very pretty!"

"My name is Betty, and we are in Maine right now," answered Betty. "You are very shiny, were you just born?"

"Why yes," replied Freddy. "I just came from the coin factory."

"Cool. I am pretty new too. Where are you headed?" Betty asked Freddy.

"I don't know where the rest of my family is. I'd like to find them."

"I'd be happy to help you find your family," answered Betty.

"Hey you two!" A voice interrupted.

"Who are you?" asked Freddy.

"I'm George, the quarter," he replied.

"Do you know this city by heart?" asked Betty.

"Of course I do! I have been around a long time." George assured Betty.

"Well, we'd love it if you could come with us," replied Betty. "We are new pennies and need someone to be our guide."

"Sure! I'd like to have some new traveling companions," answered George, and so the three coins jumped out of the pocket. The midday sun shone brightly off of their sides as they lay on the sidewalk.

"I'm rusting! I'm turning brown!" complained Freddy.

"Freddy, don't you realize that you *are* brown? All pennies are born that way," explained George with a laugh. Freddy blushed.

Laughing, the coins got up and cheerfully rolled along. They passed many houses and a beautiful rose garden. Then they rolled to the top of a grassy, green hill. There was a large and fancy fountain at the bottom. "Race you to the fountain!" George said. The coins rolled quickly down the hill, squealing and laughing. They rolled and rolled, until they reached the edge of the fountain. They were covered in mud and bits of grass. The water in the fountain looked cool and refreshing. "Whoever jumps in last is a rotten coin!" George exclaimed.

Chapter 2: The Fountain

"George, you act like such a little kid!" Betty teased.

"What's a 'fountain' anyways?" Freddy asked them, looking puzzled.

"A fountain is a fun place where coins go to cool off and hang out with each other," answered Betty.

"Then what are we waiting for? Let's go!" Freddy excitedly hopped into the fountain. George and Betty followed him. The sparkling water rinsed off their dirt and soon their sides were shining again. Looking around, they saw that there were hundreds of other coins in the fountain. They waved and introduced themselves.

"There are lots of coins I know here!" announced George with a smile. "Let me introduce you to my friends."

"Good afternoon, my name is Dompion," said a dime, with a graceful bow.

"This is my buddy Zingo," said George, gesturing to another penny. "He knows a lot about coin history. Maybe he can help you find your family."

Zingo nodded and said, "First, you have to get to the city of Sacramento. Once you are there, find the California State Capitol. Ask the governor for a half-dollar coin. The half-dollar coin can lead you to Washington D.C. to show you where to find the leader of the golden coins. He is very powerful and wise. Surely, he will be able to help reunite you with your family."

"Wow, you are so smart! Would you like to come with us, Zingo?" Betty asked.

"I would love to!" Zingo replied. "It's been a while since I went on a trip."

"Can I come, too?" asked Dompion.

"Sure!" exclaimed Freddy with a smile. "Well, well, well… what have we got here?" muttered a nasty voice behind them. Freddy and his friends flipped around to find a bunch of mean-looking coins scowling at them.

"Looks like a bunch of losers stumbled into the wrong fountain," scoffed one of the coins, a dime who was covered in scary-looking scratches.

"Um… hi, nice to meet you?" Freddy stuttered. He tried to move towards the coins, but he was frozen by some kind of magnetic field. His eyes grew wide with fear. No matter what he tried, he couldn't move. "Who are you guys and what do you want with us?" Freddy asked.

"My name is Rocky Demine," answered the tough-looking dime, "and this is my posse. We're the Awesome Possum Cool Dude Club. But the question is, who are you? If we don't think you and your buddies are cool, then you're all out of here!"

"There's only one way to find out how cool these newbies are!" announced

Pruchen Explosion, a nickel who was rough around the edges. "Cliff diving! And not from just any cliff, but the tallest cliff there is." Pruchen pointed up to the very top of the sculpture that rose out of the fountain. The sculpture was of a lady holding a rose high above her head.

"That's right," a large and tough-looking quarter called Awesome Force nodded in gruff agreement.

Rocky Demine nodded at Awesome Force, who was holding a giant magnet, and suddenly the magnetic force pushed Freddy and his friends upwards through the water. Once they broke through the water, the magnetic force kept pushing them, higher and higher, until they were at the very top of the fountain. They were perched on the edge of the stone rose's petals. Freddy peered over the edge and realized that the lady's hand and the rose extended beyond the edge of the fountain. There wasn't water beneath them, only cement!

Chapter 3: A Leap of Faith

"Please, don't hurt us!" Betty pleaded. The mean coins began to laugh evilly. Then Awesome Force moved the magnet again, pushing Freddy and his friends over the edge. Their bodies plummeted towards the hard concrete below. Betty was screaming. Freddy took a deep breath and closed his eyes. He could feel the air rushing all around his body, as he fell faster and faster, until his body smacked hard into... feathers? He opened one eye. "Am I dead?" he looked around in confusion. He, Betty, and George had landed safely on the wings of a mountain bluebird! He breathed a sigh of relief.

"Look over there!" Betty smiled, pointing sideways. Zingo and Dompion were riding on the wings of a female bluebird that was flying next to them. Freddy smiled and waved.

"Gee, thanks so much for saving us!" Freddy exclaimed, looking into the eyes of the bluebird that was carrying him. "But why did you help us when you don't even know us?"

"Birds and coins have always been allies, so whenever there's a coin in need, I'm there." answered the mountain bluebird with a friendly nod.

"Well thanks again! I'm Freddy, what's your name?" asked Freddy.

"I'm Bingo," replied the mountain bluebird. "And this is my girlfriend Ren." He waved a bright blue feather at the glossy green female that was flying beside him. "What are you shiny coins up to today?"

"We need to find transportation to Sacramento," said Betty. "Do you have any suggestions for how we might be able to get there?"

"Ren and I can fly you guys to Sacramento."

"Really?" the coins beamed at the two bluebirds happily. "Thank you so much!" They rolled up onto Ren and Bingo's backs as they soared higher into the sunny sky.

Chapter 4: Flying

Flying was very exciting for the coins. They could feel the brisk air against their faces and when they sat on the edge of Ren and Bingo's wings they could look down at all of the wonderful places they were passing. Every few states, they would stop so that Ren and Bingo could rest and eat.

In Pennsylvania, they saw the Liberty Bell and ate Dutch strudels. In Nebraska, they tasted Omaha steaks and visited the state capitol. When they reached Nevada, they went to Tahoe and Reno. It was January, so they were surrounded by snow. In Reno, the colorful lights of the casinos shone brightly at night, turning the white snow beautiful rainbow colors.

In Tahoe, they made skis for themselves out of sticks and they even used the ski lift. From a human's point of view it would have looked like just an empty seat with two birds in it, but there were really five coins in there! They spent the afternoon skiing and then it was back to flying.

Ren and Bingo flew as fast as they could, and less than a day later they landed in California!

In the coin world, there are two versions of Oakland. One is the Oakland that people know, which is full of tall buildings and concrete streets. The coin version of Oakland is a city made up of oak trees that is very close to the Russian River. They landed in the coin city of Oakland, where they spent the night in the branches of a beautiful old oak tree. The next day, Bingo bought a map from the gift store. They used the map to figure out the best way to get to the State Capitol and took off. They flew like lightning, and arrived at the State Capitol in less than an hour! The coins used the doormat to shine themselves nice and bright before rolling in through the front door.

Chapter 5: The State Capitol

"I never knew it would be so quiet and pretty." whispered Betty as she admired the enormous building.

"Me neither," remarked George in awe. "Freddy, I think you should go with Zingo. The rest of us should wait here. Too many coins rolling around might make people suspicious."

Freddy and Zingo rolled up to the door of the governor's office, then turned sideways so they could quietly slip through the crack between the door and the floor. Zingo spotted the governor sitting near the window with a bored look. "Sir Governor, we need your advice," he announced in his bravest voice.

The governor turned around and screamed, "Ahhhh! Talking coins!" His mouth hung wide open. He blinked his eyes, and then he took off his glasses. He rubbed them on his shirt and put them back on. *The talking coins were still there!* He took several long gulps of coffee.

"Um, hi Mr. Governor," Freddy stuttered. "My name is Freddy and I am looking for my family. This is my friend Zingo. He says that you might be able to help me by giving me a half-dollar coin." The governor gaped at them in shock. Then he finished the last of his coffee. Shaking his head, he got up and poured himself another cup. *I must be going crazy,* he thought to himself, *but if I give these imaginary talking coins what they want, then maybe they'll go away.*

He cleared his throat, sat back down, and tried to focus his gaze on the two tiny pennies.

"A half-dollar coin, you say? Well I've got just the thing." He opened his desk drawer and rummaged through it for a minute. Then he took out a large silver coin.

"Wow!" Freddy gasped.

Zingo grabbed the silver coin. "Thanks so much, Mr. Governor!"

The governor nodded slowly. Then his eyes rolled back and he fainted. The three coins quickly rolled out of the office.

When they got outside, they motioned to the others. The coins and birds gathered on the steps to make their next plans. The half-dollar coin introduced herself as Demytra, the leader of the half-dollar coins.

She said that she could show them the way to Washington D.C. and that she knew the leader of the golden coins personally. They were all very thankful and relieved. But what they didn't know was that Demytra was keeping a secret from them.

Chapter 6: Washington, D.C.

Demytra gave directions to Ren and Bingo and the coins hopped up onto their wings. They flew for a couple days until they saw a large billboard that said "Welcome to Washington, D.C.!" Ren and Bingo landed near a clean and cozy-looking hotel. When the hotel staff wasn't looking, they snuck into an empty room. It was humongous, and it felt like a mansion to the tiny coins and the birds! They all slept in the same big bed, and the flat-screen television was like a big movie theater screen to them! They watched movies all night until they fell asleep.

When dawn came, Zingo woke everyone up early so they could plan their visit to the White House. They ate breakfast at a nearby diner for coins. A friendly female dime took their orders, and they made plans while they ate waffles and pancakes.

As soon as their planning was finished, they paid the bill and quickly flew off. For people, it is pretty easy to find the White

House, but for coins it isn't. Luckily, they had Demytra as a guide and thanks to Ren and Bingo, they also had a bird's-eye view. They flew around the D.C. area while Demytra navigated. "There it is… the White House!" Demytra pointed proudly at the grand building ahead of them. It had four columns, a triangular roof, and a ton of steps. Ren and Bingo landed and the coins rolled off their wings, heading straight towards the White House. It was an amazing sight. They had never seen a building so grand and fancy. They hopped quickly up the steps and rolled inside.

"Whoa!" said Zingo, looking around. There were columns, crystal chandeliers, and gorgeous oil paintings. The hallways were filled with important-looking people, like guards, chefs, Secret Service agents, secretaries, and more. For a little while they all just wandered around in a daze, enjoying the luxurious decorations.

"Hey guys!" Freddy shouted. "Didn't we come here for a reason?" The others looked at him and suddenly snapped back to reality.

"Uh, yeah... haha," Zingo replied sheepishly. "We were just admiring the place. It's amazing! Sorry, back to business."

Chapter 7: The Leader of the Golden Coins

"The leader of the golden coins is on the third floor, in the room where they display valuable artifacts," informed Demytra. "Let's head in that direction." The coins followed her up a winding staircase that was carpeted in rich, blue velvet. A few minutes later they reached the room where valuables were stored. The coins slid under the door. The room was filled with glass display cases. Each one displayed priceless-looking artifacts, such as platinum necklaces and purple jewels. They searched frantically for the leader of the golden coins.

"There he is!" Freddy whispered, pointing at a glass case with a large golden coin inside. They instantly knew that this was the coin they were looking for. There were burglar alarms everywhere, but the coins were too tiny to set off the motion detectors. Freddy and Zingo grabbed a paper clip from the guard's desk, then they quietly and carefully used it to unlock the case that was holding the golden coin.

They opened the case just wide enough to let the golden coin slide out. He grinned widely at them, and then they all rolled away without making a sound. They rolled swiftly out of the White House like nothing had happened.

"Finally, I'm out of that stupid case!" exclaimed the golden coin once they were far enough away. "Thank you, brave coins. How can I ever repay you?"

"By telling us your real name and helping us find Freddy's family." Betty said.

"Wilbert is my name," he replied, "And I can definitely help you find Freddy's family…" he paused and took a deep breath. Then he motioned to Demytra, who came over and stood beside him.

"What's going on, Demytra?" Freddy asked.

"Demytra is your mother and I am your father," Wilbert said.

Chapter 8: Family

"Wh-, what are you talking about? Are you serious?" Freddy exclaimed in shock.

"Well, a long time ago, back in Maine, the coin makers used to keep all the half-dollar coins with golden coins. The golden coins were the fathers and the half-dollar coins were the mothers. Together, they had pennies for children. Then one day, the director of the coin factory gave all of the half-dollar coins to the governor of California and all of the golden coins to the president. Your mother and I were terrified about being separated, but there was nothing that we could do. You were born after we were gone. I am so sorry that we weren't able to be there for you sooner," Wilbert explained.

"You were born to be a special coin, one who would bring other coins together for adventures that would fill their lives with joy," Demytra said. "We believed that one day you would find us. I have been waiting a long time for this moment."

"Wow." Freddy said. "I can't believe I have really found my family!"

Wilbert and Demytra hugged him tightly. "We knew you would be different and special," whispered Wilbert. "You made these coins happy. And you changed their lives."

"I did?" Freddy asked.

"Yes you did. You helped these coins discover the greatness of the world around them," Wilbert said.

"It's true!" agreed Dompion.

"Yes," added Zingo. "It's been a great adventure."

"You know what would be really great? Going home. It's time we all had some rest." Dompion suggested.

"You can all come live with me if you want." George suggested to the rest of the coins.

"We'd love to!" they exclaimed. The coins hopped onto Ren and Bingo's wings and headed towards Maine.

The sun was setting and the sky was filled with wispy clouds in different shades of pink, purple, and gold. The coins sat side by side on Ren and Bingo's wings as the sun dipped below the horizon. "Ah, there's no place like home..." Freddy said in a relaxed tone as he looked up at the stars that were starting to appear. Home was a paradise that everyone could dream about, and Freddy finally had a family to share it with.

About the Author

Gabrielle Begun is an aspiring young writer from San Francisco, California. She began writing *Freddy the Penny* when she was eight, and completed it by the age of ten. Her dream is to someday see her beloved tale about Freddy be made into a screenplay.

Gabrielle is passionate about the art of writing. She organized the first writer's club at her school and has been actively running it for around four years. She is a member of the yearbook committee and was offered a job as a copywriter for the school's yearbook. In April 2013, her writing skills were recognized by the California Association of Teachers of

English (CATE) and she received a "Writer of Distinction" Award.

In addition to writing, Gabrielle also loves to read. Her favorite authors are Ralph Fletcher, Rick Riordan, Mikhail Zoshchenko, and Veronica Roth. In her free time, she also swims, plays volleyball, and rides horses. A true performer, Gabrielle also enjoys dancing, singing, and playing piano and guitar. Gabrielle's daily motto is "Don't Stop Believing."

The Lekha Way

At Lekha, we believe that children's ideas are more imaginative than those of adults. It is this imagination that Lekha Writing Center wishes to nurture and develop. By learning how to turn their imagination into words, children learn how to put their ideas on paper and become successful communicators.

Our instructors guide young writers in a supportive environment, using our time-tested creative methods. Instead of using traditional prompts, we incorporate fun activities, nature, and lively discussion to inspire each child's unique ideas. A cat that turns into tomatoes, a spider defeating a lion, or a mad scientist befriending a computer—these are just a few examples of how the Lekha Way can stimulate your child's imagination.

Lekha Publishers LLC, an independent publishing company, has been conducting after-school classes, enrichment programs, camps, and workshops for children since 2006, as part of its educational outreach department. To learn more about Lekha, visit www.lekhaink.com.